SIMON &
SCHUSTER
EDITIONS

SHE LOVES YOU

A CURIOUS TALE CONCERNING A MIRACULOUS INTERVENTION

ELAINE SEGAL
DRAWINGS BY LANCE RICHBOURG

SIMON & SCHUSTER EDITIONS
Rockefeller Center
1230 Avenue of the Americas
New York, NY 10020

SIMON & SCHUSTER EDITIONS and colophon are
trademarks of Simon & Schuster Inc.

Design by Elaine Segal and Lars-Erik Fisk

Manufactured in the United States of America

1   3   5   7   9   10   8   6   4   2

Library of Congress Cataloging-in-Publication Data
Segal, Elaine.
She loves you : a curious tale concerning a miraculous
intervention / Elaine Segal ; drawings by Lance Richbourg.
p.   cm.
I. Title.
PS3569.E39S34   1997
813'.54—dc21   97-12321
CIP

ISBN 0-684-83895-8

SHE LOVES YOU

No one could have been less prepared

for the discord of adolescence than my father and I, particularly as our relationship had been launched on such a promising note. I was his firstborn and had been greeted with the kind of tender awe a very large person often feels for a very small one who bears the stamp of his manufacture, and as soon as I got my bearings I happily returned the favor by worshipping my father and everything about him; even the air around him was improved for having been breathed by him and I gladly took this air into my body for the sheer pleasure of breathing with my father.

Then suddenly

I was transformed from an
adorable miniature person
into an alarming facsimile of
an adult and the air divided
into his air and my air and to
admit of a need for the other's
air was to invite a nameless but
nonetheless terrible defeat.

And so began
a great struggle

to prove that one's own air was the better, firmer air, which only resulted in all the air becoming polluted with mutual disapproval.

But of the mass
of things I disapproved
of about my father, it was
his disapproval of me that I
disapproved of most and even
as I was rebelling most fiercely,
I was secretly yearning to win
back my father's approval, which I
craved as much as I did my freedom.
How I could attain either of these
prizes without sacrificing the other
was profoundly unclear to me.
And then into this confusion of
cravings stepped the Beatles.

I was sitting in the front seat of my father's Pontiac,
entertaining myself with a reliable fantasy
that revolved around a
pink motorcycle . . .

. . . when my father
reached over and
turned up the radio.

And when you touch me,
I feel happy inside,
sang some men.
It's such a feeling that
my love I can't hide,
they continued.

"A forced rhyme if I ever heard one," said my father. "I don't see why these Beatles are supposed to be so much better than our American groups. Do you?"

"I don't see what the big deal is," I said, in a tone meant to convey that the world had insulted me personally with yet another of its brainless enthusiasms.

But I did see what the big deal was. I saw it right away. When the Beatles jubilated, *I can't hide! I can't hide!*, what they meant was, *I won't hide! I don't have to hide!* And what they didn't have to hide from was my father's opinion. The Beatles would understand that, for the moment, I had to hide.

They'd know that my betrayal was in the cause of the greater good; that it was the strategic first step in coaxing my father out of the lengthening shadows of his day into the high noon of mine, where a person could have some fun.

Into this bright picture came rolling a vision of the Beatles,
riding through the neighborhood in a lost limousine.

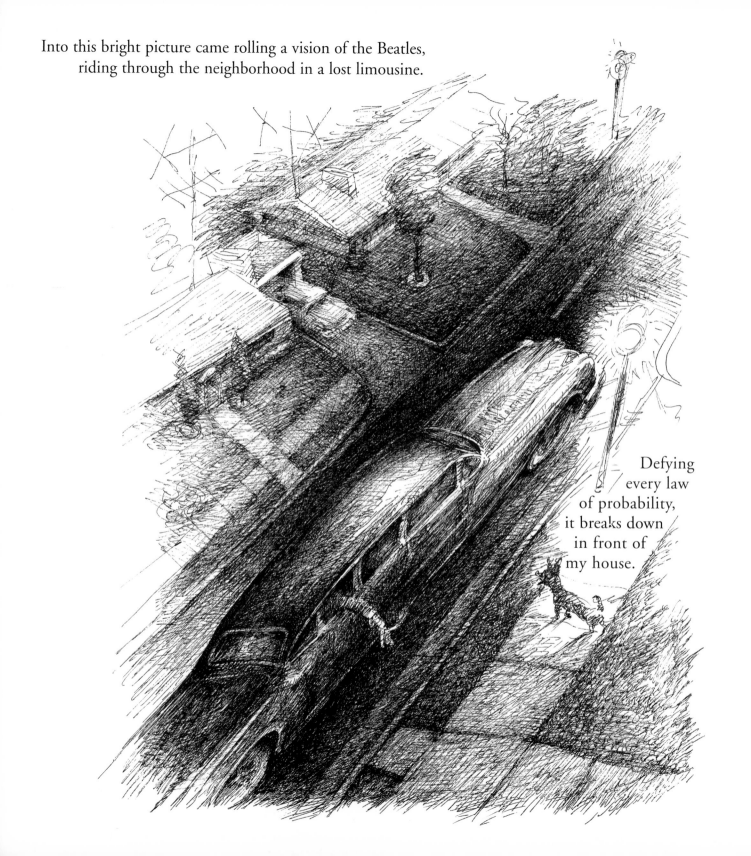

Defying
every law
of probability,
it breaks down
in front of
my house.

Who needed a pink motorcycle
when one had at one's disposal
the dazzling potentiality
of a lost limousine?
How much better to animate
one's hope-crazed teenage mind
with four undauntable,
saucy knaves whose charm
was so potent it could dissolve
every objection to them,
the way Coca-Cola
was shown to dissolve teeth
in a science project.

But

just as those teeth
didn't dissolve overnight,
neither would my father's
skepticism. I knew that. And so, as time
went by and the Beatles became supernaturally
famous, I continued to affect disdain while every so
often slipping in an interesting fact sure to awaken
my father's affinity to them. For instance, wasn't it *interesting* that
the Beatles used a cello in "Yesterday"?

"Yeah, yeah, yeah," said my father. "Pretentious is more like it."

Oh. Well, what I meant was, wasn't it *interesting* that for all
their pretension, the Beatles had taken on such a humble soul as
Ringo, so cheerful in the face of criticism of his drumming, not
to mention his sickly childhood and recent tonsillectomy?

"A *man* who wears *jewelry? Feh!*" was all my father would say.

Oh. Well, what I meant was, wasn't it *unusual* for a rock group
to have an intellectual in it, like John?

"Mick Jagger went to the London School of Economics," my father pointed out.

Still, I hoped on.

Every night as I sat at the dinner table half listening to my father's predictions of what would and what would not become of me, I waited for the doorbell to ring.

"Who could that be?" my mother would say.

"Probably one of her good for nothing boyfriends," my father would reply. *"I'll take care of it."* He throws down his napkin, advances to the front door, and flings it open.

"We're sorry to disturb your supper, sir," says Paul,

"but I think we've blown a gasket!"
He points to the disabled limousine
in front of the house, piles of
steam billowing out of its hood.

"And we're lost," puts in Ringo, pointing to the chauffeur, who is peering into a map with a frowning expression.

"I wonder if we could use your phone," says John.

"That is, if it isn't too much trouble," says Paul.

"No," says my father quietly, in shock from the Beatles' good manners, "it wouldn't be any trouble. Come in."

"Ahhh,"

says Paul, striding into the living room and stretching his arms out, "It's been such a long time since we've been in a real home. It does a body good, eh, lads?"

"That it does,"
says George.

My father catches my eye
and nods with approval.

"You boys must be hungry,"

he says. "Why not have a bite to eat?"

"**Oh, no,** we couldn't impose," says Paul.

"It's no imposition," says my father. "You must eat to live!" he adds, philosophically.

"My kugel!" exclaims my mother . . .

"Oh, well, we want to live, don't we, lads?" says John, sincerely yet sarcastically.

. . . and dashes into the kitchen.

"Ahhh," says Paul, "it's been such a long time since we've had a nice noodle kugel. Would you be needing any help, mum?" he adds, considerately.

"**I hope** you boys don't mind your kugel a little crispy," my mother says, apologetically.

"That we don't,"
says George.

"I don't like
the sound of
that cough,"
my father tells Ringo.

"Oh, it's nothing," says Ringo. "Just a touch of me old pleurisy acting up. Nice doggy," he adds, bending down to pat the dachshund, who gives out a groan of pleasure and falls on her back. My father lifts an eyebrow. "She usually doesn't take to strangers," he says, respectfully. "Just a case of underdogs of a feather, mate," says Ringo, winking.

"Well, what are you boys waiting for?"
my father says, heartily.

"Eat!"

The Beatles
dig in.

"Isn't this good,"

John remarks, regarding a forkload
of kugel. "It reminds me of . . .
Norwegian wood."

"Nor-wee-gian wood," sings Paul.

"Would you have a bit of paper and a pencil?" John asks me.

As my father and I look on,
John writes "Norwegian Wood."
    "Amazing," murmurs my father,
"straight out of his head with
no cross-outs!

Just like Mozart!"

While the Beatles are in the
kitchen helping my mother with
the dishes, my father gives me
his confidential opinion of them.

Of Paul:
"Heck of a nice guy."

Of Ringo:
"Very touching."

Of George:
"Don't under-estimate him. Still waters run deep."

And of John:
"I didn't know . . ."

I go to my room to pack my bag.
When I come out, the Beatles
are lined up at the front door.
John and my father are locked
in a long, manly handshake.

"Goodbye, Dad.
Goodbye, Mom," I say.
"My baby!" cries
my mother.
"Don't worry about
her," my father says,
gruffly. "She knows
what she's doing."

Hundreds of kugels

came and went during the age of the
lost limousine fantasy, and it so
happens that the last dinner
I ate before I left home
for good was, in fact,
kugel.

Desperate to save me

from the fate he imagined lay in store,
as the kugel sat untouched in the center
of the table, my father prophesied the
destruction of my body and soul with
such imaginative detail, it was clear
that this was not the first time he
had entertained the scenario.

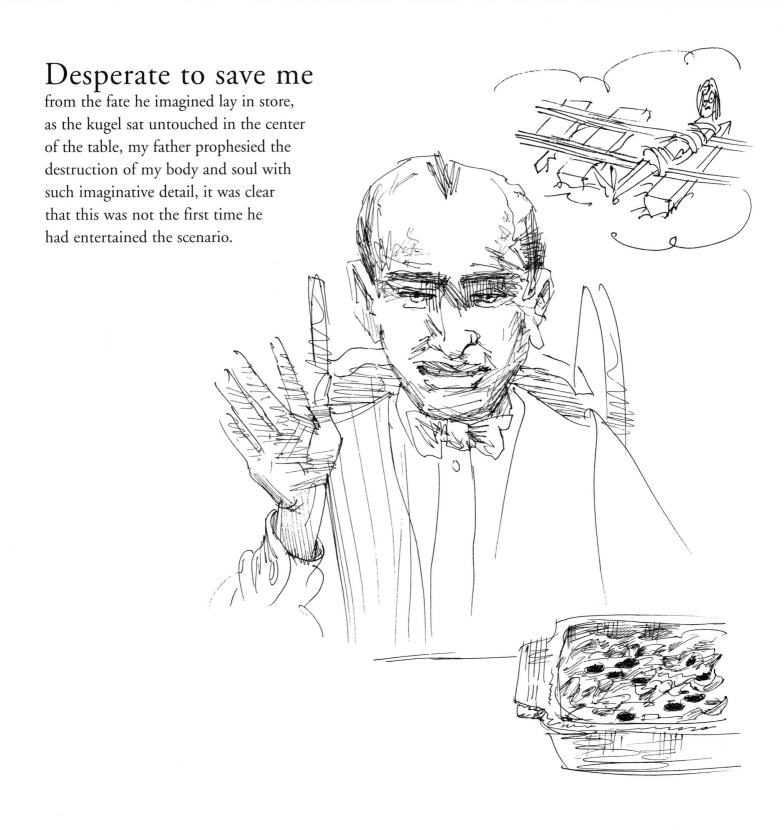

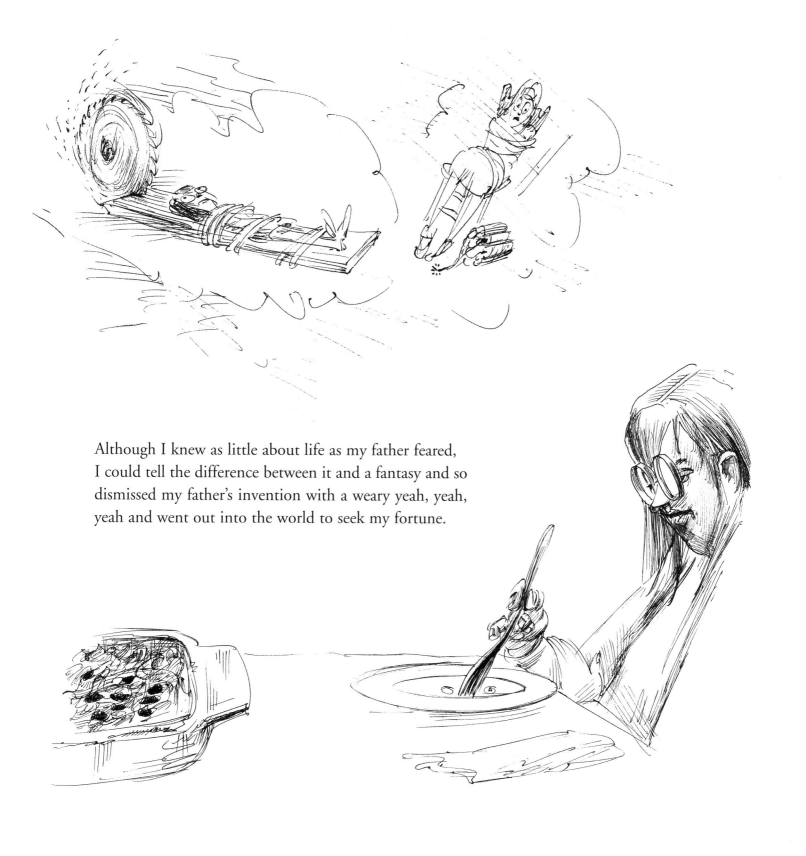

Although I knew as little about life as my father feared,
I could tell the difference between it and a fantasy and so
dismissed my father's invention with a weary yeah, yeah,
yeah and went out into the world to seek my fortune.

Maybe in some parallel universe I come to my senses at that last supper and cry,
You're right, Dad! You're always right! Tell me what to do and I'll do it!

Or maybe in some other unknown area of reality, the ruined air between my father and me is restored by a miraculous visitation of the Beatles.

But in the only universe

I know about, I neither surrendered
nor have, as yet, come to a bad
end as a consequence,

and if my father has gained any affection
for the Beatles, he has not had
occasion to mention it.

We have, nevertheless, achieved a realistic, if flawed, peace, which I confess I still dream of perfecting:

As my father lies
on his deathbed,
the Beatles come to
pay their respects.

"Who is it?"
my father
asks weakly.
"It's the Beatles,
Dad," I say.
"Good, good,"
says my
father.
"I'd hoped
they'd
come."

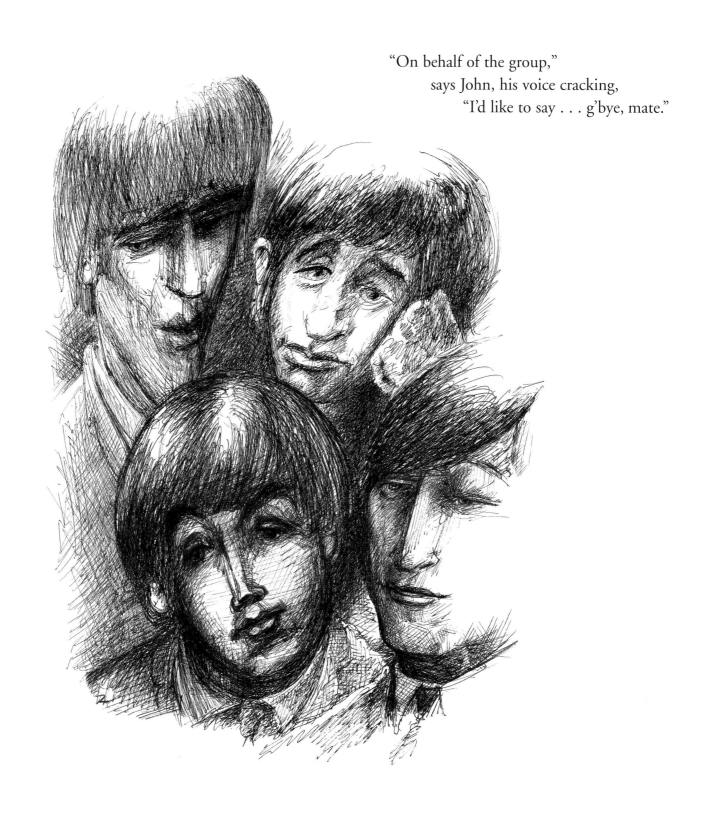

"On behalf of the group,"
  says John, his voice cracking,
    "I'd like to say . . . g'bye, mate."

I nod
to the Beatles.
Very quietly, they
set up their instruments
and play an acoustic version
of "She Loves You" at half tempo.
Beckoning me close with a shaky,
gnarled finger, my father breathes his last
words into my ear. "You know," he whispers,
"Ringo . . . really was . . . a good drummer."